My 1st Classic Story

Rumpelstiltskin

a retelling of the Grimm's fairy tale

by Eric Blair

illustrated by David Shaw

PICTURE WINDOW BOOKS

a capstone imprint

My First Classic Story is published by Picture Window Books
A Capstone Imprint
151 Good Counsel Drive, P.O. Box 669
Mankato, Minnesota 56002
www.capstonepub.com

Originally published by Picture Window Books, 2004.

Printed in the United States of America in North Mankato, Minnesota.
032010
005740CGF10

Library of Congress Cataloging-in-Publication Data
Blair, Eric.
Rumpelstiltskin : a retelling of the Grimms' fairy tale
retold by Eric Blair ; illustrated by David Shaw.
p. cm. — (My first classic story)
Summary: An easy-to-read retelling of a classic tale in which a
strange man spins straw into gold, asks a huge reward, and
offers a seemingly impossible way out of the deal.
ISBN 978-1-4048-6079-7 (library binding)
[1. Fairy tales. 2. Folklore—Germany.] I. Shaw, David, 1947- ill.
II. Grimm, Jacob, 1785-1863. III. Grimm, Wilhelm, 1786-1859.
IV. Rumpelstiltskin (Folk tale) English. V. Title.
PZ8.B5688Ru 2011
398.2—dc22
[[E]]   2010003630

Art Director: Kay Fraser
Graphic Designer: Emily Harris

The story of *Rumpelstiltskin* has
been passed down for generations.
There are many versions of the story.
The following tale is a retelling of the
original version. While the story has
been cut for length and level, the basic
elements of the classic tale remain.

Once upon a time, there was a poor man who bragged to the king. He said his daughter could weave straw into gold.

The king led the girl into a room filled with straw.

"Weave this straw into gold by dawn, or you will die," the king said.

The girl had no idea how to weave straw into gold. She cried and cried.

Suddenly, a tiny man appeared.
"Why are you crying?" he asked.

"I don't know how to spin gold from straw,"
she said.

"What will you give me if I spin it for you?" he asked.

10

The girl offered her necklace. The little man spun all the straw into gold.

When the king saw the gold, he wanted more.
He took the girl to a much bigger room.

Again, the funny little man appeared.

"What will you give me if I spin the straw for you?" he asked.

This time, the girl offered her ring. The little man spun all the straw into gold.

The king wanted more. He took the girl to an even bigger room.

"If you can spin all this straw into gold, I will make you my wife," he said.

That night, the funny little man came again. "What will you give me this time?" he asked.

"I have nothing left," said the girl.

"Then when you are queen, you must give me your first child," the little man said.

The girl did not know what else to do, so
she agreed. The tiny man spun the straw
into gold.

When the king saw the gold, he married the
girl. She was now queen.

One year later, the queen had a baby. She forgot about her promise.

But the little man did not forget. He came to the queen and said, "Now give me what you promised."

The queen offered the little man all the riches in her kingdom.

"No," the little man said.

The queen cried so much, the little man
felt sorry for her.

"If you can guess my name in three days,
I will let you keep your baby," he said.

The first day, the queen guessed all the
names she knew.

"That's not my name," he said.

The second day, the queen guessed the most unusual names she knew.

"That's not my name," he said again.

That night, a messenger saw the little man
dancing around a fire.

"Tee-hee, ha-ha, it's really such a shame that no one can guess Rumpelstiltskin is my name," the little man sang.

The messenger hurried to tell the queen.

The next day, the little man asked,
"What is my name?"

"Is your name Rumpelstiltskin?" the
queen asked.

"How did you know?" cried the little man.
He was very angry. Rumpelstiltskin stamped
his foot so hard that he disappeared into the
ground. He was never seen again.

The End